Missing Her

Missing Her

Brenda Chapman

Anna Sweet Mysteries
GRASS ROOTS PRESS

We acknowledge the financial support of the Government of Canada.

Canada

Produced with the assistance of the Government of Alberta, Alberta Multimedia Development Fund.

Government

Library and Archives Canada Cataloguing in Publication

Chapman, Brenda, 1955–, author
     Missing her / Brenda Chapman.

(Anna Sweet series)
ISBN 978-1-77153-010-1 (softcover)

     I. Title. II. Series: Chapman, Brenda, 1955– . Anna Sweet mysteries.

PS8605.H36M57 2017   C813'.6   C2017-902441-8

Printed and bound in Canada.

For Steve and Lorraine Chapman

CHAPTER ONE

A cold north wind was blowing snow into my face as I trudged toward my PI office in Hintonburg. Six days before Christmas and the city was a sparkly snow globe of icy white. Red and green lights flashed *Merry Christmas* in Gino Roma's pizza shop, to the left of the stairs that led to Storm Investigations. I wanted to be in the holiday mood, but so far I was feeling like the Grinch—green, grumpy, and sick of listening to never-ending Christmas carols in malls and restaurants.

Five shopping days left to the big day and I hadn't bought one gift. I was seriously considering booking a flight south and disappearing Christmas Eve.

Bah humbug.

The door at street level and our office door at the top of the stairs were both unlocked. I found my partner, Jada Price, working at her desk with a glass of what looked like egg nog within arm's reach. Nutmeg and a cherry floated on top of the creamy white liquid.

She was humming "Santa Claus is coming to town…" but stopped when she saw me in the doorway.

"Gino sent up some rum nog," she said, pointing to the fridge. "Help yourself."

"A bit early in the day, isn't it?"

"Never too early for some cheer." She studied my face as she lifted her glass and toasted me. "Did Nick make his flight okay?"

"He did. I expect he's landing in New York City as we speak."

"And he's gone until New Year's?"

"Work before pleasure."

Jada shook her black dreadlocks. "I don't understand the movie industry."

"They're filming Christmas scenes and want to use the New York backdrop while it's decked out for the holidays."

"Still." She took a long swallow of egg nog. After a twenty-second pause, she said, "A man named Albert Romaine is arriving shortly and I'm hoping you can meet with him. I have an apartment viewing in an hour."

"Any information about Romaine?"

"Not really. He said it was about a cold case when he called. Nick took the message and started a computer file before he left yesterday."

I was quiet for a moment. Nick still liked working in our office when he wasn't on a film shoot. But his acting reputation was growing and he was in demand. He likely wouldn't be working for us much longer. I shrugged out of my coat, sat down at my desk, and opened the Romaine file.

Albert Romaine hadn't given Nick more than an address and phone number. He lived in Orleans, an Ottawa suburb that was sixteen miles east of the downtown. Nick's note said that Romaine wanted to meet us before giving any more details.

The secretive type, I thought. I leaned back in my chair and watched the snow swirling outside the window.

"What kind of movie?" Jada asked.

I turned my head. "Movie?"

"Nick. You know—in New York."

"Oh. Romantic comedy."

"I thought Nick hated those."

"Carolina Mambella is his co-star. She begged him to take the part. Their last movie together was a big hit. The movie critics say their on-screen chemistry is remarkable." I tried to sound happy about that.

"I'm sure Nick could co-star next to a turnip and they'd say the same thing. He's one gorgeous hunk of man." Jada stood up quickly and grabbed her parka from the coat rack on her way to the door. "I hope this apartment in the Glebe is decent. Henry and I have to move by the end of January."

"Will your brother be able to stay in the same high school if you leave your neighbourhood?"

"I don't see why not." She bent down to put on her boots. "Especially if I don't tell anybody. Let me know how it goes with the Romaine guy. The case is all yours if you decide to take it. I plan to take next week off for Christmas and to start packing for the move."

"An old cold case might be just the distraction to get me through the Christmas holidays," I said.

I decided to put off booking a ticket south, until after I found out what Romaine wanted.

....

Albert Romaine arrived twenty minutes after Jada clumped down the stairs. He was a large, out-of-shape man with sandy hair cut short in the back with a long swoop of bangs that fell across one eye. I placed him in his mid- to late twenties. He had a square jaw and piercing blue eyes that took in the office, and me, before he crossed the room to sit in the visitor chair. We shook hands before he sat down.

"Can I get you a coffee, tea?" I asked to kick things off.

"No, thanks." He took a deep breath. "How good are you at finding people?"

"We've found a number of missing people. Who are you searching for?"

"My fiancée, Shelley Vincent. She disappeared over a year ago and the police have stopped looking." He looked down at his hands folded in his lap. His right knee was jumping up and down, the only sign that he was upset.

I tried to recall if I'd heard about his missing girlfriend but nothing came to me. "Do you think she's come to any harm?" I asked.

His head shot up. "God, I hope not. The cops have no idea what happened to her." His eyes met mine. "I was out of town when she went missing and they ruled me out as a suspect."

"Were you getting along before she left? Were there any signs she was unhappy?"

A flash of anger crossed his face before his mouth relaxed into a smile. "We were very happy together.

And no, I didn't see any signs of anything wrong before I went to Toronto that week on business. She called her mother and sister after she took me to the airport, then went to work later that day and the next morning. Nobody noticed anything off."

"Why were you angry just now?" I asked.

He raised both hands, palms skyward. "I've been grilled by the police about our relationship, as if I must have done something to her. I'm frustrated that I'm the only suspect they looked at, when I'm innocent. In my opinion, they didn't try hard enough to find her. Before or after they ruled me out."

"I can start today if you'd like to hire us. I have a standard contract ready to sign. It states our hourly rates."

"Yeah, I'm fine with paying whatever it takes. It would be good to have her home for Christmas ... or at least to know what happened to her. I haven't been able to move on."

"Christmas is only a few days away, but I'll do the best I can. I'll need a list of people in your lives, where you both work, and other information. We can start with this questionnaire."

"Whatever you want. She means the world to me and it's killing me not knowing if she's okay."

··········

An hour and a half later, Albert had told me all he could about his missing fiancée and their life together. He gave me his cellphone number and asked that I call him if I found out anything, no matter the time, day or night. He looked out the window before leaving.

"Bad driving tonight," he said. "Are you on the bus or did you drive in?"

"Drove. I've got a parking spot behind the building."

"Good snow tires?"

"Not really. It's a loaner and has all-season tires."

"You really need good winter tires in this weather."

"Yeah, I plan to visit the Chevy dealership when I have a free day."

"Well, take it easy on the way home."

I sat sorting through my notes long after he'd gone and began outlining my interview list. Albert had met Shelley in college when they were both twenty-one, some four years earlier. They'd been engaged and living together for more than two years before she disappeared. Shelley had a business certificate and helped manage a Tim Hortons coffee shop in the east end. Albert was a computer programmer working for the government.

He'd given me a photo of her before leaving: Shelley standing in the kitchen, looking up at him as he snapped the picture. She was of medium height and build with long brown hair and hazel eyes. Pretty, but not a woman who would stand out in a crowd. She had a startled look in her eyes, as if Albert had surprised her, but I couldn't detect any other emotion on her face.

Albert had snapped the picture the morning that she drove him to the airport. "It was taken in the last hour that we were together," he'd said as he handed the photo to me. "I keep looking at it, trying to figure out what was going on in her head."

I stood and stretched before checking my watch. Nearly five o'clock and darkness had settled in. I crossed to the window and craned my neck to see the street below. The snow was falling faster and the road was bumper to bumper with barely moving traffic. I decided against visiting Shelley's workplace at the other end of the city, but I'd stop at the Elgin Street police station on my way home.

Albert had given a copy of the police report to me, and my soon-to-be-ex brother-in-law Officer Jimmy Wilson's signature was scrawled across the bottom. He and my sister Cheri had been living apart. She'd filed divorce papers a month earlier, and last I heard, he hadn't signed them. Hopefully, I'd catch him before he left for the day. Jimmy and I had a history that included being engaged before he dumped me for Cheri.

With any luck, he wouldn't hold a grudge against me for turning down his offer of getting back together the last time I'd seen him. That was about as likely as seeing reindeer fly across the sky pulling a sled full of toys.

CHAPTER TWO

The desk officer told me to sit in the waiting area after he called Jimmy to report my arrival. Usually Jimmy invited me right in, so this was new. Forty-five minutes later, the officer told me that Jimmy was ready for me in his office.

Let the games begin.

Jimmy was on the phone with his back to me when I took the visitor chair across from his desk. He raised his pointer finger above his head to let me know that he'd be a minute.

"Okay," he said into the phone as he turned to face me. "Deliver it to the station on Elgin and give my name at the front desk." He hung up.

"Police business?" I asked.

"Could say. What brings you here this cold winter evening, PI Sweet?"

I studied him for a moment. The lines around his eyes suggested a lack of sleep. His face was greyish in the bright overhead light. "How are you, Jimmy?"

"Never better."

"I'm sorry for how it turned out . . . with Cheri."

"All for the best in the long run. She's found a new man who appears to suit her more than I did. You have, too, for that matter." He smiled, but it was a sad smile. "I'll get over it, Sweet."

"You haven't been to visit Dad."

"I needed distance from your family. In fact, I'm flying to Cuba for a Club Med vacation later tonight."

"But Evan will miss you over the holidays."

"Cheri has him until New Year's Eve. The new reality." He picked up the stapler and squeezed it hard. "So why are you here?"

"I have a new client named Albert Romaine. His fiancée's been missing for more than a year and you investigated her case. Do you remember?"

"Yeah. Shelley Vincent. We cleared her boyfriend, Albert, since he was out of town with a lot of witnesses to his whereabouts that week. I concluded it was a suicide because her wallet and credit cards were left behind. No clothes were taken either, and there was no action on their joint bank account. We'll probably find her body in some remote wilderness location one of these days."

"Did she have a car?"

"She had a driver's licence. But they only had one car so Albert usually dropped her off at work and picked her up. The car was in the driveway."

"How would she have gotten to the wilderness, then?"

"We think she used a bike. Albert said she didn't own one but she could have bought one with cash if she was planning this. He said she'd talked just the week before about getting a bike to get around the city."

"So, you never actually located a bike."

"No, but we'll likely find it when we find her bones."

I was silent, taking a moment to process what Jimmy was telling me. "Albert said that she was happy and he didn't have any idea why she left. Did anyone you interviewed notice signs that she was depressed?"

Jimmy shook his head. "Nobody had much to say about her state of mind. She was busy with work and getting ready for their wedding. I think it would be best if you talk to her family and friends yourself and get your own take. Maybe I missed something that you'll see with fresh eyes."

"Okay."

We stared at each other. I knew he didn't want my sympathy and I couldn't think of anything to say that wouldn't come out sad. He dropped the stapler onto the desk and stood up.

"I'll walk you out."

We talked about nothing important on the way to the front entrance. The desk officer waved Jimmy over as we started down the corridor. He was chatting with a young man who had his back to us.

The officer said, "Your delivery is here, Wilson."

The young man turned and said to Jimmy, "Cash or credit?" He was holding a large pizza box in one hand and a credit card machine in the other.

"Police business, eh, Officer Wilson?" I said. I put my arm across his shoulders and gave a quick squeeze. "Merry Christmas, Jimmy. Enjoy your trip south."

Jimmy reached out an arm and hugged me back. "You're welcome to join me in Cuba," he said as he started walking toward the desk. He turned without stopping and grinned. "No strings attached."

"Sounds inviting, but no thanks."

I stepped outside into a foot of new snow and a cold wind whipping around the building. Dad was getting ready to fly to Florida to spend the holidays with his lady friend Betty. The storm would be over by December 23, when he was to fly out. Everyone was going south, it seemed. Dad, Jimmy—even Nick, although New York wasn't exactly a tropical getaway. I didn't know what Cheri and Evan had planned but I imagined they would be going somewhere warm too, with her new boyfriend. I'd be the only one left in Ottawa. I didn't mind, though. Not really. December 25 was just a day on the calendar. No more or less important than any other day.

· · · · · · · · · ·

Dad was in the kitchen pulling a pot roast out of the oven when I got home. He set the pan on the counter and wiped his forehead with a dish towel as I turned down the volume on the radio. "Jingle Bells" faded into the background.

"You're home," he said. "I thought you'd be here a lot sooner."

"New case. Roast smells delicious."

"I'll serve it up if you open the bottle of red wine on the table."

"Deal."

I walked into the dining room and saw the table set for three. "Is someone else joining us?" I called to Dad as I wrestled with the cork.

"Yeah, call Evan to wash up. He's in the spare bedroom reading."

I walked to the bottom of the stairs and called up to my nephew. He appeared on the landing, his hair sticking up in tufts and his sweater on inside out. He jumped down the steps and gave me a hug.

"You're getting so tall, buddy," I said rubbing the top of his head.

"Catching up to you," he said before slipping past me. "Sit down Aunt Anna and I'll help Grandpa serve supper."

"You know that I love you to bits, right?" I asked as I followed him back into the dining room. Even with all the craziness going on between his parents, Evan was one terrific seven-year-old kid. He'd become very attached to my dad, spending a lot of time at our house.

We ate slowly and caught up on each other's news. I found out that school was out for the holidays and

Evan was staying with us until Christmas Eve. Cheri and her boyfriend were on holiday in Barbados for the week.

"A last-minute decision," Dad said quietly when Evan had gone to the kitchen to get ice cream and bowls. "Evan didn't want to go with them so I offered."

"What is *wrong* with her?" I asked, not expecting an answer.

Evan yelled from the kitchen. "You bought the chocolate cookie dough kind, Grandpa!"

Dad held my stare. "Because I knew it was your favourite!" he called back.

·········

Later, after we'd eaten and Dad took Evan out in his truck, I sat at the desk Dad had set up for me under a window and read through Jimmy's notes. Shelley's mother, Grace Vincent, lived in the Vanier neighbourhood of Ottawa. Her younger sister, Rosemary, appeared to be at the same address. The father, Denis Vincent, lived in Oakville, near Toronto, with his second wife. The file contained their phone number. All good contact information, if nobody had moved since the last round of interviews.

Grace would be my first stop in the morning. It was interesting that she'd kept her married name after the divorce, but I didn't think it meant anything to the case. She might have wanted to keep the same last name as her daughters.

While I'd been working, Dad and Evan had come home and soon after, Evan went to bed. I found Dad in the living room screwing a Christmas tree into a stand in front of the window.

"I wasn't going to bother but Evan wanted a tree," he said. "We're going to decorate it tomorrow if you're around. We'll also be baking cookies."

"Probably not, Dad. I'm working on this case. By the way, what does Evan want for Christmas?"

"His parents back together." Dad gave a sideways frown. "Since that won't happen, I got him some books and a telescope." He stood back to look at the tree. "Straight enough. How about you pour us each a Scotch to help us unwind before bed?"

"I was about to suggest the same thing," I said, "proving once again that great Sweet minds think alike."

CHAPTER THREE

The next morning, I cleared the snow off my car and dug out the end of the driveway before I got underway. Happily, the snow had stopped falling and the sky was satin blue instead of filled with grey clouds. Bright sunshine sparkled on the snow and reflected off the windshield. I found my sunglasses at the bottom of my bag and put them on before I backed my car onto the street.

I took the Queensway across the city to Vanier in the east end, where Shelley's mother and sister lived. Albert and Shelley lived a bit further east in Orleans. Orleans and Vanier once had been cities on their own but now both were part of Ottawa. People who lived there had been mainly French-Canadian but the population was changing.

I drove through neighbourhoods until I reached Ethel Street. It was a poorer part of town with a mixture of low-rise apartment buildings and small, single-family homes. Grace and Rosemary Vincent lived in a run-down bungalow wedged in between two narrow houses with stucco walls and flat roofs. A plastic blow up Santa took up the entire front yard.

The curtain in the living room window lifted and dropped as I waded through the knee-deep snow to the front steps. The door opened before I had a chance to knock. An overweight girl who looked about twenty years old stood in front of me. She had wavy long red hair and held a baby doll tucked into the crook of her arm.

"Mom is out," she said, her blue eyes openly studying me from head to toe.

"Do you expect her home soon?"

"Yes. Would you like to come in?"

"If that's okay."

"Follow me."

She led me down the hallway, past the kitchen to a small room that had been set up as a nursery. More dolls were sleeping in carriages and lay lined up in a crib. The girl rocked the doll she was holding before she placed it on the change table.

"I was just putting my babies to bed," she said. "You're very pretty."

"Why don't I wait outside?" I asked, taking a step backwards. "I don't want to disturb ... anyone."

The front door opened as I started down the hallway.

"Rosie, I'm home! Did someone come to the door?" The woman saw me and stopped.

"Rosemary let me in, Grace," I said quickly. "I didn't realize ..."

Her anxious face relaxed. She had the same red hair as Rosemary but cropped short. She was slender and wore jeans and a grey hooded sweatshirt under her parka. "It's okay, except I keep telling her never to open the door when I'm not here. She and I will have a chat about that later. Do I know you?"

"My name is Anna Sweet. I'm a private investigator. Albert hired me to try to find your daughter Shelley." I pulled my ID out of my pocket and held it in front of me at eye level.

"You'd be the second one, then. Would you like a cup of tea?"

"If it's not too much trouble."

"No trouble."

She led me into the kitchen and I sat at a small table while she checked on Rosemary. She returned a few minutes later and put on the kettle. "Rosie is too busy with her kids to join us," she said, smiling. "She pretends that she's running a daycare. You likely noticed that she's much younger mentally than her age."

"She seems like a lovely young woman."

"Thank you."

After Grace filled the teapot and got cups from the cupboard, she sat down across from me. "Now, what's this about finding Shelley?"

"Albert hired me yesterday because he said he needs to know what happened to her. I've read the police report and met the lead investigator."

"That would have been Officer Wilson. He told me that he believed she killed herself."

"What do you think?"

"There was a time I would have said she'd never do something like that. She had a good job and was getting married. She was busy that year and we didn't see much of her, but she called now and then. Usually on a break at work. She kept saying that she'd get over to see us." Grace wiped a hand across her eyes. "But she never did. I guess I didn't know what was going on with her at the end. Maybe it's true that she took her own life. I just wish I knew why."

"If she did, I'll try to find out for you." Grace poured the tea and I added milk. "How were Shelley and Albert getting along?" I asked.

"Good." She paused. "At least she never said if they were having problems."

"Have you stayed close to him?"

"We weren't ever that close. He calls now and then to ask if I've heard from Shelley."

"So he thinks she's still alive?"

"I'm not sure if he does or if he can't let go of the past."

"You mentioned that I wasn't the first PI that Albert hired."

"That's right. He hired a firm soon after Shelley went missing but they didn't find her."

I finished my tea without learning anything more than I'd read in the report. Rosemary was singing a lullaby to her dolls as I followed Grace down the hall to the front door.

"Rosie's always so happy," said Grace as she opened the door. "No matter how bad things are, she brings a smile to my face. Sometimes she even makes me forget that I've lost Shelley—at least for a little while."

•••••••••••

Since I was already in the east end, I drove to St. Laurent Boulevard to stop in at the Tim Hortons where Shelley had worked as assistant manager. It was nearing lunchtime but early enough that the place wasn't too busy. I knew that in half an hour all the seats would be filled.

I was in luck. The manager, Rudy Brown, was on shift and agreed to sit with me for a few minutes to talk about Shelley. Rudy was in his mid-thirties, dark-haired with a bushy moustache and beard. His dark brown eyes studied me sadly after he set his cellphone on the table. "Not a day goes by we don't miss her," he said. "She was quiet but a good worker and had a way with the customers. She was also very smart about the financial part of the business. I relied on her to keep the books straight."

"Can you tell me about the last time you saw her?" I asked.

"Sure. Her boyfriend was in Toronto on business so she worked late that night and then came in around ten the next morning, which was June 10. We were busy that day and I was surprised that she asked for the afternoon off. She said that she wanted to take advantage of her future husband being away."

"Were those her exact words?"

"Yup. I thought she was going shopping or getting her hair done or something personal. I had no idea she meant to kill herself." He looked down at his hands, which were folded on the table next to his phone.

"Is that what you think happened to her?"

"What else could it be?"

"Did she have any friends on staff or customers she talked to often?"

"Nobody she spent any time with outside work." He thought for a moment. "The police and the other PI never asked about customers before. This old guy Joe used to have a coffee with her now and then. Kind of an odd dude. Long grey hair and always dressed in plaid shirts."

"Do you have his last name?"

"No. He doesn't come in as often anymore. He pays cash when he does. Maybe he gets the money panhandling."

I reached into my pocket and pulled out a business card. "Next time you see him, would you call me right away?"

"Yeah, I could do that."

"Maybe don't tell him that you've contacted me."

"A surprise attack?"

"You could put it that way. I'm worried that he might not want to talk if he gets advance notice."

"I understand."

Rudy's cellphone lit up and beeped. He picked it up. "Sorry, one of my staff texting to let me know she's going to be late. Tina Fellows. You might want to speak to her too, actually. She worked the same shifts as Shelley."

"How late is she going to be?"

His phone beeped a second time. "That was Tina again. Looks like she won't be in today at all. Her kid is sick and her sitter just cancelled."

I stood. "I'll check in with you tomorrow and will come by to speak with her if she's working. Maybe I'll get lucky and Joe will be dropping in for coffee, too."

Rudy jumped to his feet. He raised his hand and called across the room for somebody to clear the leftover trays from a table. "You never know," he said, turning back toward me. "But Shelley's been gone for over a year so I guess there isn't really any rush, is there?"

CHAPTER FOUR

I returned to the office in Hintonburg by late afternoon and found Jada sitting at her desk with her feet up. She held a full bottle of beer on her stomach.

"I was hoping you'd drop by," she said.

I took a beer out of the little fridge and pulled over my chair to sit beside her. "And why was that?" I asked, putting my feet on the desk next to hers.

She clinked her bottle against mine. "To toast my new apartment. Henry and I will be moving in January 1."

"That's great." I thought about the awful apartment they were in now and the high crime in their neighbourhood. There'd been two shootings since the summer. "You're moving on up."

"Or at least to a street without a drug dealer on every corner. So, I'm hoping you don't mind if we skip Christmas dinner with you this year. Henry is in Montreal with some friends until Christmas Eve and then we need to pack and clean up enough to get our deposit back."

"No problem."

My Christmas party was now down to me—not that I planned to have one. There wouldn't be many dishes to clean up afterwards in any event.

"Any progress with the Shelley Vincent case?" Jada asked, nudging my foot with hers.

"No. I'm talking with people from her life." I swallowed a mouthful of beer and thought for a second. "She was secretive. Nobody appears to know what she was thinking or how she was feeling that summer."

"Is that in the report?"

"Only if you read between the lines. I don't know if she was involved with someone or something that got her killed."

"So you don't buy the suicide theory?"

"Not yet. I might in the end though, just like Jimmy did."

"Maybe you'll be able to track down her movements that last day and find her body."

"Not the best outcome, but better than it sits now. Her mother and Albert will continue suffering until they have closure."

"Yeah, all that waiting—hoping and dreading at the same time—can be a real killer."

I nodded my agreement. "It's always better to know, no matter how terrible the news."

••••••••••

Evan and Dad were sitting down to eat when I arrived home. Dad had a plate warming for me in the oven and I joined them after pouring a glass of red wine from the bottle on the counter.

"Nothing fancy tonight," Dad said. "Pork chops, homemade applesauce, and latkes."

"Latkes are just fried potato pancakes," said Evan with his mouth full.

"Good to know," I said.

"How was your day?" Dad asked.

"Interesting." I took a sip of wine. "Would you be available to do some research, Dad?" I asked. Dad's previous work in the military made him first-rate at tracking down information.

"Of course. What's your new case about?"

"A missing woman named Shelley Vincent. I have a short list of family and people in her life I need you to check out."

"I'll get on it first thing tomorrow."

"She's been gone for more than a year and might have," I looked at Evan's bowed head, "you know, done herself in. But her boyfriend and mother want to know either way."

"Understood."

After supper, Dad and I went over the list in my office while Evan watched television. Then the three of us put on our parkas and boots and went for a walk through our Alta Vista neighbourhood to look at Christmas lights. A gentle snow was falling and the night air was cold but not as frigid as it had been.

"Five days until Christmas," Dad said.

"Three days until you fly to the sunny south," I added.

"Maybe Aunt Anna and I could fly with you, Grandpa," said Evan. "Then we could be together."

Dad looked at me over Evan's head. "Your mom will want you with her for Christmas," he said, "and I'll only be gone a week."

"A week's a long time." Evan picked up a chunk of icy snow and heaved it at the stop sign.

"In the history of time," said Dad, "one week is really just the blink of an eye. We'll be back together before you even have time to miss me."

CHAPTER FIVE

I went for a jog as the sun was creeping up over the houses the next morning. Dad's cooking had been turning me into a buttery lump until I started working with a trainer the month before. I'd toned up, lost ten pounds, and was feeling better than I had in months. Pie and biscuits were still in my meal plan but so were jogging and regular visits to the gym.

On my return home, I slowed to a brisk walk as I passed by Nick's house, next door to my dad's. Nick had big plans to fix up each room but had barely set foot inside after closing the deal. I saw tire marks in the driveway and wondered who'd been parked there recently. It had to be within the last day or the marks would be filled in with freshly fallen snow.

Curious.

Evan and Dad were still sleeping when I stepped inside the back door. I drank a glass of water and then showered and dressed for the day in jeans and a warm pullover. Afterward, I took a bowl of yoghurt and berries into my office and found the phone number for Shelley's dad, Denis. It was nearly nine o'clock when I dialled the Vincent phone number in Oakville. Three rings later, a woman answered. She said that I'd only missed Denis by ten minutes.

"Could you please pass along my name and phone number to him and ask him to phone me this morning?" I asked, after explaining why I'd called.

"I'll give you his work number," she said. "It's a general number at the Canadian Tire and you can have him paged. I'd wait half an hour, though, to be sure he's arrived. He stops at the Starbucks for coffee on his way."

So much for worrying about his privacy.

I brewed a pot of coffee in the kitchen and poured a cup while I waited. Evan was moving around upstairs and I heard him cross the floor to the bathroom. Dad turned on the radio in his bedroom and the muffled voice of a newscaster came through the ceiling. I returned to my office and tapped in the Canadian Tire phone number. A pre-recorded message walked me through five minutes of choices with key-punching before a real person came on the line. She immediately put me on hold, and store ads played in my ear for another ten minutes.

"Yeah, hello," a man's deep voice finally growled in my ear.

"Denis Vincent?" I asked.

"It is. Do I know you?"

"No. My name is Anna Sweet and I'm a private investigator. Your daughter Shelley's fiancé, Albert Romaine, hired me to try to find her."

Silence.

"I'm wondering if you've heard from her this past year or have any idea about where she might be."

"Are you kidding me? He's going to drag this all up again?"

"Excuse me?"

"It's crystal clear that my daughter went off somewhere and killed herself. We don't need to relive that time. Him least of all."

"I'm sorry if this is upsetting. If she *is* dead, Albert wants me to find her body to give her a proper burial."

"Well, finding her is a long shot after all these months. I'll be amazed if you can pull it off, since the police and that other PI couldn't. But don't get me wrong. Nobody would be happier than me if you find out what happened to her."

"When was the last time you saw or spoke to Shelley, Mr. Vincent?"

"Not sure. She'd stopped calling after she met Albert. She used to come visit twice a year, but that stopped too, after a while."

"Was she upset about something?"

"Not that I could think of. I guess she got busy with her job and new boyfriend ... excuse me, *fiancé*."

"If she decided to leave Ottawa, can you think of anywhere she might have gone?"

"Nope. I wish I had some bright idea or insight to share, but I don't. Sorry."

I thanked him for his time and hung up. I looked at the frost on the window as I thought about Shelley's relationships. She'd been withdrawing from her family the year before she vanished. Had she been growing more and more depressed and nobody had noticed? Even Albert hadn't seen the signs, unless he hadn't wanted to see them.

My line of vision landed on my cellphone and I saw a message waiting sign. I picked up the phone and clicked on the screen. I counted three messages from Albert the evening before. And he'd phoned twice while I was on hold with Canadian Tire. He had to have something urgent to tell me. Worried, I hit his number. He answered on the first ring.

"Albert, you've been trying to reach me. Has something happened?"

"Happened? No. I wanted an update."

"What?"

"I want to know if you've found anything."

"I've only just started. I have nothing to report to you yet." I couldn't hide the surprise in my voice. He'd phoned me what, five times for an update?

"I know. I'm sorry. It's just that I've been so desperate to find her."

I used my patient but firm voice that I kept for frantic clients. "I've been on the job less than twenty-four hours, Albert. As soon as I know something new, I'll be sure to call you."

After a short pause, his voice regained control. "I'd expect nothing less. Contact me anytime, day or night. I'll be waiting for your call."

. . . .

Jimmy's police file included the name and cellphone number of Shelley's best friend. Elle Chambers had been working overseas when Shelley went missing. From what I could tell, Jimmy had never interviewed her. I called the number and was rewarded when Elle answered—she was back in Ottawa. She agreed to meet me in an hour for coffee at Morning Owl Coffeehouse on Bank Street.

The sun was fully up but struggling to shine through the cloud cover when I drove downtown. The low clouds were keeping the air slightly warmer than the day before—the only benefit from the depressing gloom.

I parked in a lot and paid the fee rather than driving around downtown searching for a free spot. Elle was already sitting at a table drinking a large coffee and eating a muffin when I arrived. I recognized her from the description she'd given over the phone: long dark hair and black eyes, dressed in jeans and a red parka. But she hadn't told me how pretty she was, which I noticed when she flashed a wide smile my way. I waited in line for a coffee and joined her a few minutes later.

"Thanks for meeting me," I said.

"Happy to finally talk to someone about Shelley," she responded. "I've been back in town a month now but didn't know if I should contact anyone."

"You were working overseas?"

"Yes, as a waitress in Scotland. I got to travel and see the world. I couldn't believe it when I heard Shelley was gone."

"The police tried to reach you."

"So I heard later. I was surprised to get your call this morning."

"Shelley's fiancé, Albert Romaine, hired me to find her."

"Find her body, you mean. Her mom said the police figured she killed herself."

"Maybe. Probably. But I'd like to bring her home if so."

Elle swiped at a tear that had fallen onto her cheek. She hunched forward, both hands wrapped around her coffee cup. "How can I help?"

"Tell me when you first met Shelley and what she was like."

"Shelley and I were in some of the same classes in high school. She was smart and funny and generous. She helped me pass math and I helped her fit in. She was shy and awkward but when I was with her she came out of her shell. She loved her mother and sister, swimming, movies, books, and good coffee. I didn't hear from her much after I'd been in Scotland for six months or so. She stopped emailing me and I got busy with work and travel. I'm so sorry I wasn't there for her. I feel as if I let her down."

"Did you meet Albert?"

"Yes." Elle lifted her cup and drank.

"What did you think of him?"

"I told Shelley not to settle. But she said he loved her and she was happy."

"Why did you say not to settle?"

"He was her first real boyfriend. She was smarter than him ... by a long shot. Sure, he was great with computers, but not much else as far as I could see. He never got her jokes and he didn't read books. He was good at sweeping her off her feet, though, what with all the flowers, jewelry, and trips to romantic inns. Still, I thought she could do better."

"But she said that she was happy?"

"Yeah." Elle shrugged. "More than once."

"Did she have any favourite place in the woods or near water that you can think of? Someplace she might go to be alone."

"And end it all? No, I can't think of anywhere. She wasn't into nature that much." Elle looked at me with a haunted expression in her eyes. "All through high school, we dreamed about going to Europe together. I begged her to come with me, but she said that all she wanted was to marry Albert and have children. The worst thing is that none of her dreams came true in the end. I wish I knew what changed to make her so sad when I was overseas. I wish I'd been a better friend."

CHAPTER SIX

I drove west out of the downtown to my office in Hintonburg. Gino waved me inside his pizza shop as I walked past the window. I loved the tomato-basil-garlic smell every time I stepped into the restaurant, and today it made my stomach grumble.

Gino hugged me and stepped back to study my face. "You're wasting away," he said. "Sit while I make you a special pepperoni pizza. I'll double the cheese."

"Well, if you insist."

I sat on a stool at the counter and watched him work. After he tucked the pizza into the oven, he poured two glasses of iced tea. He set one in front of me and sipped on the other.

"So, heard from Nick since he went on the New York shoot?"

"Not so far, but it's only been two days. What are you doing for Christmas, Gino?"

"Visiting family in Toronto. I guess you'll be with your dad and sister?"

"I'll be busy," I said, without actually agreeing. I didn't need him to pity me.

We chatted about the holidays and the weather until my pizza was cooked. Then I went outside and climbed the stairs to my office. The place had that deserted feel, with Jada and Nick away.

I returned some phone calls and sorted through emails sent to our business's address. One made me smile and I opened it first. Nick had sent me some photos of the locations where they were filming the movie. He said that he was working long hours. He missed me and would call soon.

I was humming as I updated the Shelley Vincent file. I liked to make notes after every interview, to read over each evening. Sometimes, a detail I didn't think meant anything could become important later. Dad called as I was finishing my last entry.

"I've researched a couple of names from the list you gave me," he said. "Shelley Vincent's father is in charge of purchasing for the Canadian Tire in Oakville. He and Grace divorced when Rosemary turned five and Shelley was ten. He married his second wife, Valerie, a year later. Valerie is a real estate agent and grew up in Toronto. Denis and Valerie do not have any kids."

"Interesting. Anybody else?"

"I looked into Albert Romaine's family history as you asked. Albert grew up in Cornwall on a farm. His mother died when he was eight and his father, Pierre, raised him and his brother, Guy."

"Where are they now?"

"Pierre died of cancer two years ago. The brother, Guy, is married and running the farm. He has three daughters and sixty dairy cows."

"Albert chose computers over farming."

"Looks that way. He won awards in school for his computer skills. I didn't come across anything else of note. No hobbies or social groups outside of work that I could find."

"So, he and Shelley didn't belong to any organizations, like church or sports teams?"

"No."

"Well, good work, Dad. I'm going to do a bit of Christmas shopping and I'll be home late."

"I haven't had time to cook anything so grab a bite along the way. I promised Evan I'd take him to that hamburger place he likes. We might go see an early movie."

"Okay. Have fun you two, and stay out of jail."

· · · · · · · · · ·

I'd just put a new set of stainless steel cooking pots for Dad into the trunk of my car when my phone rang.

"Hey, is this Anna Sweet?"

"It is." I heard background noise and someone talking very loudly behind him.

"This is Rudy Brown at Tim Hortons. You were in yesterday."

"Hi, Rudy."

"You said to call when Joe came in. He's at the counter now, getting a sandwich. I told the girl to take her time making it."

"Thanks, Rudy. I'm on my way."

"Tina's working the late shift so she'll be here too."

I drove as quickly as I safely could to the Queensway, which would take me across the city. Perhaps Joe would have some insight into Shelley's state of mind that others had missed. I could only hope.

CHAPTER SEVEN

Luckily, traffic was lighter than normal. I arrived at the Tim Hortons twenty minutes later. An Ottawa driving record if there ever was one.

Rudy was working behind the counter but he saw me standing in the doorway. He pointed toward a table in the corner and I looked over. A man in a blue plaid shirt had his back to the door. His grey hair was tied back in a ponytail. I crossed the floor and stopped in front of him.

"Joe?" I asked.

He looked up. I hadn't expected the intelligence in his dark eyes or the quick way he seemed to assess me. He must have liked what he saw because he smiled and said, "I don't believe we've met, but yes, I'm Joe."

"I'm Anna Sweet, a private investigator. Do you mind if I sit down?"

"No, have a seat."

I unzipped my jacket and pulled out the chair. The tables were small and our knees touched when I sat. I apologized and moved my seat back a foot. Joe watched me with a half-smile on his face but he waited for me to speak first.

I tried not to be flustered by his steady stare. I said, "I'm trying to find a woman who used to work here. I'm told she sometimes sat with you and talked."

"Oh?"

He wasn't going to make this easy. "Shelley Vincent. She left without making contact with her family over a year ago. She was assistant manager here."

"Shelley. Yeah, she took a few coffee breaks with me."

"How did you become friends?" He seemed like a curious choice for Shelley to have chosen for her coffee buddy.

"I don't know. We got chatting and shared a joke. I invited her to join me one slow morning, and we sat together now and then when she had time."

"What did you talk about?"

"The weather, politics, books. She had a great sense of humour."

"Did you share anything personal?"

"Not that I can recall. We weren't that kind of friends. I knew she was getting married but that was about all she told me about herself. I thought she'd moved on from this Tim Hortons after she tied the knot. I wasn't aware that she was missing."

Something in his voice didn't ring true. Was it possible that he hadn't known she was missing? According to the police file, her disappearance had been in the newspapers and on the nightly news.

I looked at him more closely. He was in his fifties but his arms were muscular and he appeared in good shape. His jeans and plaid shirt were clean and he was wearing new leather work boots. The parka hanging over the back of his chair was down and expensive-looking. I'd thought from how Rudy had described Joe that he was on the poor end of the scale. Rudy was either a bad judge of character or Joe had come into some money.

"What's your last name, Joe?" I asked.

"Does it matter?"

"I need to have it for my report."

"You never said who you were working for."

"The family." For some reason, I didn't want to share information with this guy. I added, after a pause, "Her mother and sister are having a hard time not knowing where she is. They miss her."

"I can imagine." He looked down at his hands. They didn't look toughened by labour as I would have expected. "My last name is Costa. Joe Costa."

"What do you do for a living, Joe?"

"I'm semi-retired. Construction. We have an office on St. Laurent near the Dairy Queen." He gave me a half-smile. "Look, I'd like to help you locate Shelley, but I got nothing. I'm also late for a meeting, so I'm going to have to leave." He stood and grabbed his jacket. "I hope you find Shelley and bring her home safe and sound. She's a nice lady."

He was out the door before I'd gotten out of my chair. His quick exit made me want to follow him, and I would have, except a young woman in a Tim Hortons uniform was coming toward me. She was dark-skinned with short purple hair and a worried look in her eyes.

"I'm Tina," she said. "Rudy told me to come talk to you about Shelley."

"Please sit," I said, and she dropped into the chair that Joe had just left.

"Oh that feels good, to get off my feet," she said with a sigh, before her face turned serious. "Have they found Shelley's body?"

"No, and we're not sure she's dead. Can you tell me what you know about her?"

"Well, we worked together the last year she was here. She trained me and was very patient and so funny." Tina frowned. "Shelley didn't share much about her personal life, though. I knew she was getting married."

I was beginning to see a trend in Shelley's relationships. She kept her true self private and covered her sadness with humour. "Do you think she was happy before she disappeared?"

"I guess. I can't say I noticed if she wasn't."

I asked Tina a few more questions but she didn't have anything new to tell me. I gave my business card to her before buying a toasted bagel and a Boston cream doughnut. Dad would not have approved of my supper choice but I was hungry.

It was going on seven o'clock when I finally stepped outside and headed on my way home. My cellphone rang as I was clearing a new sprinkle of snow from my windshield. I didn't recognize the number and decided to answer.

A woman's voice asked, "Anna Sweet?"

"Yes."

"This is the Civic Hospital. Gino Roma was brought in by ambulance twenty minutes ago, and he's asking for you."

CHAPTER EIGHT

I rushed across the city, worry filling my belly. The nurse on the phone wouldn't tell me what happened, although she did say that Gino was stable. Whatever that meant.

I found him in one of the examination rooms in Emergency. He was propped up on a pillow with a big bandage across his forehead. His left eye was turning purple and his wrist was bandaged, too.

"Good Lord," I said. "You look like you've been in a fight. Are you okay, Gino?"

"You think I look bad," he said grinning. "You should see the other guy."

I moved closer to the examining table. "What happened?"

"Some kids knocked over that sign on the sidewalk, the one promoting my pizza specials. So, when I went outside to set it back up, I heard a noise like breaking glass coming from the door to the stairs to your office. I looked over and saw someone pushing the door open so I yelled and started after them. They'd shattered the glass and I'd only just stepped inside when they slammed me against the wall. Then they hit me with something like a hammer, but I blocked most of the impact with my arm. I must have blacked out because next thing I knew, I was lying on the sidewalk surrounded by people. The ambulance came soon after and here I am."

"That's terrible." I took his free hand and rubbed it with both of mine. "What did the doctor say about your injuries?"

"Minor concussion, so they want to keep me overnight. My wrist is badly bruised but not broken, so that's good. Would have been hard to flip pizzas with my arm in a cast."

"Oh, Gino, I'm so sorry."

"I'll live. You should call the landlord to get new glass put in the door. Do not tell Nick about this. I don't want him worrying when there's nothing he can do."

"What about your restaurant?"

"I called my nephew Dino and he's locking up tonight. He'll work the shop tomorrow and then we'll close for three days over Christmas. I'm still going on my trip as planned."

"I won't tell Nick, but I really think you should, Gino."

"Not until he's home. I wanted to warn you, Anna. You need to take care. This person was going to break into your office and they meant business. You could have been hurt ... or worse."

I left Gino and drove back to the office. Jada was on the sidewalk talking with our landlord and two police officers when I arrived. The thick chunks of broken glass were still in front of the door.

Jada pulled me aside. "The landlord is going to get a new door tomorrow, probably a metal one instead of the glass. The police will keep an eye on our place tonight. I checked upstairs and the office is secure. How's Gino?"

"He has a concussion. He's staying in the hospital overnight so they can watch him. I feel sick about what could have happened to him."

"Not just him." Jada gave me a worried look. "Do you think this has to do with the case you're working on?"

"Maybe. I've talked to a lot of people and might have stirred something up." Joe Costa was the first person who came to mind. "The only things we have of value are our computers and the beer."

"There's still a carton of rum nog in the fridge," said Jada. "I know that's what I'd be after." She gave my arm a squeeze. "Seriously, Anna. You need to take care. I'm on standby if you need back-up."

"Good to know, partner. I'm hoping that Gino scared the person off for good. But I'll be extra careful, just in case they try something again."

Jada shivered inside her down jacket. "Getting colder," she said. "Would be nice to go south for the holidays. Too bad Henry and I are busy moving into our new apartment."

I nodded. "If I can wrap up the Shelley Vincent case, I might just consider heading that way myself."

CHAPTER NINE

I had a restless sleep. Images of Gino's battered face haunted my dreams. I woke at six a.m. unsettled and exhausted. I wondered what kind of person would take aim at somebody's head with a hammer.

After a hot shower, I dressed in jeans and a warm pullover. When I entered the kitchen, Dad was standing at the stove frying bacon and scrambling eggs. He glanced at me as I poured a cup of coffee.

"You look rough this morning, kiddo. Trouble sleeping?" he asked.

"I saw every hour on the clock all night long." I took a drink of coffee and leaned against the counter. "Can you help me track someone down today, Dad?"

"Most certainly. I'm driving Evan over to a buddy's house after we eat so I have nothing but time."

"I'll update my files and we can talk when you get back."

After we'd eaten and Dad and Evan left, I loaded the dishwasher. I turned on the radio to listen to the weather report. The announcer called for freezing rain mixed with sleet starting after lunch. Driving and walking were going to get a lot less pleasant and I had to get a move on.

I sat down at my computer and finished typing my notes into the Vincent file before beginning a search for Joe Costa. It didn't take me long to find the construction business where he worked on St. Laurent Boulevard. There was only one near the Dairy Queen and it was called Timber Construction. The ad said they built modern houses that were good for the environment. They had offices across Canada in all the major cities and some of the smaller ones. Joe might be a carpenter but my bet was that he worked in the office.

Dad arrived home from dropping Evan off at his friend's house just as I was putting on my coat.

"I wrote Joe Costa's information on a piece of paper on my desk. Find out anything you can about him—family, home address, any arrests, job history. Give me a call when you have something. I'm going to his workplace now to talk to his boss and coworkers."

"I gather you'd like something before you talk to this fella. That doesn't give me much time."

"Joe's probably not in today. He said that he's semi-retired. You can text the information to me whenever you find something. I'll keep my phone handy."

"You got it. Why don't you take one of my trucks? They both have new snow tires and four-wheel drive. The weather is turning nasty. It's also a good idea to run them, which I don't do enough in the winter."

"Thanks, Dad. The tires on my loaner car aren't the best."

"So I noticed. You should trade that car in for a more winter-ready model."

"I'll call the dealership when I get a chance."

"And I'll sleep better."

· · · · · · · · · ·

Timber Construction was a two-storey log building that took up most of a block near the Dairy Queen. A parking lot was at the east corner of the property and I found a spot in visitor parking. My phone buzzed as I was getting out of the truck. I looked at the name and saw that Albert Romaine was phoning. I thought about letting him go to voice mail but figured he'd keep calling.

"Hi. Anna Sweet here."

"It's Albert. I'm ... uh ... in my car and wondering where you are."

"I'm tracking down somebody who knows Shelley."

"Do you want to meet and you can update me?"

"No, I have nothing worth meeting about. I'll send a report to you next week if I don't find her before then. I have to go. I'll be in touch if I find anything." I clicked off my phone as he was starting to say something. He wasn't my first impatient client and I knew not to feed into his anxiety.

The inside of Timber Construction was as well built as the outside. The interior walls were reddish brown cedar logs and the floor was made of wide pine planks. A cheery log fire was blazing in a stone fireplace to the left of the entrance.

A young woman in a red plaid shirt and jeans greeted me from behind the counter. "Welcome, and how can I help you?"

I took out my ID badge and set it in front of her. "I'm trying to track down someone and I believe he works here. His name is Joe Costa. Do you know him?"

She blinked, then laughed. "Are you joking?"

"Not at all."

"Joe does more than work here. He owns the business, which has offices across the country. He's in today. Would you like to speak with him?"

It was my turn to blink. "Joe Costa owns Timber Construction?"

"Yes, he does." She turned as she spoke and I heard footsteps coming down the hall. A moment later, Joe Costa was standing next to her.

"Anna Sweet. We meet again," he said when he spotted me.

The girl smiled at him. "This woman is here to talk to you. Do you have a few minutes to give her?"

"Not a problem. I was ready for a break."

He motioned for me to follow him down the hall to his office, which was smaller than I would have expected. It was the size of a large walk-in closet and held his desk, computer, and two chairs. The screensaver was a photo of Joe on a snowboard halfway down a mountain. His long grey hair was loose and blowing behind him in the wind. We sat down and our knees brushed again as he rolled his chair around to face me.

"I hope this isn't becoming a thing," he said with a grin as he rolled back a foot.

"You didn't mention that you *owned* the company," I said.

"It's not something I usually talk about, especially with people I've just met. Anyhow, my job wasn't why you wanted to speak to me, as I recall. Any leads on Shelley?"

"A few." I had none but wanted to see how he reacted.

He smiled as if he didn't believe me. "Well, that's great. You're outdoing the police if you find her after all this time."

"Fresh eyes," I said, not taking mine off him. I would have bet my PI licence that he had something to do with Shelley's disappearance. However, a gut feeling was not proof of a crime.

"I dropped by to see if anybody knew you. But I see how foolish that looks now."

"Extremely foolish. I'm more respectable than you imagined." His smile turned serious. "I would never have hurt Shelley. I wasn't attracted to her and she had nothing I needed."

"Then I guess I'm wasting my time."

"I guess you are ... unless you're interested in building a timber home." He flashed another self-assured grin in my direction.

I knew then that he wasn't going to give anything away. I stood in one quick motion and looked down at him. "I hope you're telling me the truth, Mr. Costa. But I can't help thinking you're keeping something from me. Call it a feeling, but it's one I get when I'm being played. And I feel like I'm being played now. Be assured that I'm not done looking for Shelley—or her body. I will find out what you're hiding from me and the police. I owe that much to Shelley's family, who miss her more with every day that goes by."

I waited a moment for him to respond. But he sat as still as a statue with a strange look on his face. Like a cross between regret and worry. I dropped my business card onto his desk and said, "Call me if you remember anything that could help me to find her."

I left Timber Construction without answers but with the knowledge that I'd wiped the smug look out of Joe Costa's eyes.

And with the strongest feeling that I'd better keep checking behind me for trouble.

CHAPTER TEN

I stopped to check on Evan's gift on my way home. It would be ready for pick up Christmas Eve and I bought other supplies that I'd need. The freezing rain started as I pulled into our neighbourhood. The clock on Dad's dashboard read four o'clock, so the bad weather was a few hours later than predicted. One small bit of good luck in my day.

I found Dad and Evan in the kitchen icing gingerbread cookies and listening to "Deck the Halls" on the radio. Dad gave me an odd look from under his bushy eyebrows. He waited until Evan was taste-testing a cookie to pull me aside.

"I didn't want to scare Evan, but somebody was parked outside the house before you came home. The person drove off after you got out of the truck. I know because I was keeping an eye on them."

"What time did they arrive?"

"Not sure, but the car was there an hour ago when I first looked."

"Are you certain they were watching our house?"

"I saw the same car earlier in the day, around lunchtime. I got my coat on to check it out, but the person sped off when I opened the front door." Dad's face was regretful. I knew he would have liked to get his hands on the driver.

"Did you see their licence plate?" I asked.

"The car had tinted windows and I never got a good angle on the licence plate. The car was a four-door, black."

"What the heck is going on, Dad? Someone tries to break into our office and now someone is watching our house? The Shelley Vincent case is over a year old, so can this even be connected?"

"How many people have you interviewed?"

"Her mom and sister, people at work, her father ... I think I know who could be behind this but I have no idea why. And I have no proof."

"Then you need to be very careful, Anna." He paused. "I could cancel my trip."

"Definitely not. I'll be fine, Dad. Cheri will be back in town Christmas Eve and Jada is on call. There's nothing to worry about."

"I sure hope you're right."

"I can handle whatever the week has in store. You go and sun tan by the ocean as planned."

"If you're sure." His eyes showed he was worried. "I made some notes about Joe Costa for you. He lives in Vanier. He is not married and has a long-time girlfriend. His company is worth half a billion dollars on paper. He keeps his name out of the news. He was arrested thirty years ago for smoking pot at a rock concert when he was in his twenties. Nothing illegal since then."

"Hmm. Not what I was expecting."

"What were you expecting?"

"A more violent history, maybe. Someone who might be capable of swinging a hammer at Gino. Well, thanks anyway for looking, Dad."

Dad scratched his head and said, "Maybe this Joe Costa's simply good at covering his tracks."

"Maybe."

··········

The next day, I stayed close to home and hung out with Evan while Dad packed for his Florida trip. He was still uncertain about going and I wanted to make sure he didn't back out because of me. After a quick soup and sandwich supper, Evan and I drove Dad to the airport in his truck for his seven o'clock flight. The freezing rain had stopped and flights were on time. We helped Dad with his bag and hugged him goodbye at the escalator that would take him to the lower level and security.

"Remember, Evan, I'll be home in the blink of an eye," Dad said, as he gave Evan a hug.

"And you take care," Dad ordered me, before turning away.

Evan saw me salute my father's back and laughed. "Grandpa likes to tell you what to do, Aunt Anna."

"Always has and always will."

I took Evan's hand as we walked toward the entrance. I felt as if someone was watching us, but couldn't spot anyone staring our way. The hair on the back of my neck was standing on end and I told myself to ignore the feeling. My body was in nervous mode because of everything going on.

"Let's go right home," I said to Evan. "I'll make popcorn and we can watch a movie."

"Can I pick?"

"You can."

If anybody followed us on the trip home, I never spotted them. Once inside the house, I double-checked that all the doors were locked. Then Evan and I snuggled up under a blanket on the couch to watch *Finding Nemo*. I forgot all about the case and the break-in for the next few hours. After the movie ended, Evan got ready for bed.

I made a final check of the doors and windows and took a long look at the street before climbing into bed. I was asleep before my head hit the pillow.

CHAPTER ELEVEN

The house phone woke me early Christmas Eve morning. I leapt out of bed and scooted into the kitchen to answer before it went to voice mail.

"Oh thank God!" Cheri cried across the miles of telephone wire. "I was so scared you'd be gone. Is Evan with you?"

"He is but he's sleeping."

"I need to know if Dad left for Florida."

"He left yesterday. What's going on, Cheri?"

"We can't get off this island today. There's a hurricane warning and flights are cancelled."

"Are you safe?"

"I think so. I was lucky to get through because phone lines could go down any minute. Jimmy's not answering his phone. Can you keep Evan until I reach him?"

"Jimmy's in Cuba. Of course I'll keep Evan." I didn't like the idea of telling him that his mom wouldn't be home today. He was going to be so disappointed.

"I hope we make it back tomorrow. I'll be in touch."

"Don't worry about Evan."

"Thanks Anna. I'm going to owe you big time."

I hung up the phone and stood looking out the kitchen window. The sun was only beginning to send slivers of pink light through the darkness. A wind was rattling pings of frozen rain against the glass. What was that expression? *Red sky in the morning, sailors take warning.* Looked like another bad weather day ahead.

"Who was that, Aunt Anna?"

I looked toward the doorway. Evan was standing there in his Batman pajamas, staring at me.

"Your mom is stuck in Barbados because of a storm. She'll try to get a flight home tomorrow but no guarantee. It looks like it's you and me today, buddy."

His smile surprised me. "That's okay. Can I help with your new case?"

"I'm going to put the case aside for the day. How do pancakes sound for breakfast?"

"Great! I can make the batter. Can we add chocolate chips?"

"That's the only way I know how to make them."

We got busy and I turned on holiday music while

we cooked and ate. Despite my plan not to celebrate Christmas, my morning with Evan was putting me into the mood. We were deciding whether to go skating or sledding when I heard my cellphone ring on the counter. The caller had a private number. I clicked on it anyway.

"Anna Sweet? This is Joe Costa."

A surprise to say the least. "Why are you calling, Joe?"

"We need to meet. I have something important to share with you about Shelley."

"Should I be worried?"

"No, I don't believe so. Are you able to drive to Carleton Place this morning? We can meet at the Starbucks on the highway in, say, an hour and a half."

I took a few seconds to respond. "Two hours."

"Okay, and Anna?"

"Yes?"

"Make sure you aren't being followed."

I hung up and went in search of Evan, who was upstairs getting dressed. I needed to phone his friend's mom to make sure he could visit for a few hours. I had no idea what lay ahead in Carleton Place, a growing town forty-five minutes west of the city. Joe's last warning made me cautious.

This time, I picked the truck that Dad kept in the garage, remembering that he'd asked me to drive both when I got the chance. A longer drive would warm up the engine and get the oil flowing.

· · · · · · · · · · ·

I drove a few side streets to make certain nobody was following me before I took the on-ramp to the Queensway. I exited without signalling, watching to make sure nobody cut off the highway with me. All looked good and I pulled into the Starbucks parking lot in Carleton Place only five minutes late for the meeting.

Joe Costa was sitting at a table near the windows and he watched me enter. I went to sit down across from him but he raised a hand to stop me. "Are you sure you weren't followed?" he asked.

"I'm sure."

He pointed to a woman in a black jacket sitting near the back entrance. "Shelley's waiting for you."

I'd run through several scenarios in my head on the way to Carleton Place, but this was not one of them. I crossed the floor to sit across from her. "Shelley Vincent?" I asked, but I already knew it was her. She'd cut her hair short and dyed it blonde but her eyes and face were the same as in the photo.

"Alive and well," she said. "I'm only here because Joe said you weren't going to quit looking. You need to stop or you're putting us in danger."

"By us to you mean you and Joe?"

"No, Joe is helping us. He gave me an accounting job in one of his offices in another city. He's paid for me to start a new life. By us, I mean my daughter and me."

"I'm confused."

"This isn't easy to talk about."

"I'm not here to judge you."

She took a deep breath. "Albert Romaine is not the nice guy he appears to be. You need to know that."

I'd felt something off about Albert and wasn't as surprised as I might have been. Still, I needed proof that what she was saying was true. "Can you give me some examples?" I asked.

Shelley closed her eyes for a moment. When she opened them again, they were filled with pain. "We were good together at first. But that changed. During the last few years of our relationship, he called me every name under the sun and made me feel useless. He was controlling and jealous. He timed how long

Brenda Chapman

it took me to drive home from work and got angry if I was a minute late." Her eyes kept looking past me toward the door. She took a deep breath.

"He took my pay cheques and decided how much money to give me. He made sure I didn't have any friends or activities outside our apartment. He even stopped me from seeing my mother and sister and visiting my father. I had to sneak phone calls to my mom from work. If I hadn't met Joe, I don't know what would have happened to me and my baby. Joe saved us." She grabbed onto my hand. "Albert must never find out about Lulu. I named her Lulu because my sister, Rosemary, calls her favourite doll that name." She smiled for the first time.

All the while that Shelley was talking, her eyes were darting past me to the windows and at whoever entered the coffee shop. I could see that Joe was watching too. I felt a chill pass through me even with my warm parka on.

"Why do you think he would follow me here?" I asked.

Her frightened eyes met mine. "He's very smart about computers and technology. He uses tracking devices and cameras and can get past spyware into someone's computer."

The warning signs began slotting into place.

Albert had asked about my car the first time we met. I'd told him it was a loaner in the lot behind our office building. He had time to plant a tracking device. He must have been thrown when I drove Dad's truck instead of the car two days ago. No wonder he called to set up a meeting when I was at Timber Construction. He was trying to find out where I was. He must have been waiting outside our house for me to arrive home and saw me pull up in the truck.

He might have had time to put a tracking device on the truck I used yesterday. But he couldn't have known about the second truck in Dad's garage.

I tried to sound confident. "I'm in my father's truck today. Albert wouldn't have known about it."

She shivered. "Otherwise, he'd be here."

I remembered the attempted office break-in. Albert must have been trying to get to our computer. I thought about how viciously he'd swung the hammer at Gino.

"Did Albert ever hurt you?" I asked.

"At the end. He twisted my arm and punched me in the shoulder. I was scared he'd hit me in the stomach. I was pregnant but never told him. I recorded him on my cellphone yelling at me and throwing me around. Audio not video."

"We could get him on assault."

"I want to come home and see my mother and Rosemary. They should meet Lulu before she gets any older. I feel awful making them worry. I was hoping Albert would find somebody else and it would be safe for me to make contact. When Joe told me that Albert hired you, I knew he wasn't letting go."

"Albert went at a friend of mine with a hammer when he was caught trying to break into my office. If I can get evidence, I'm going to press charges."

"If he's locked up, I could see my mother."

"Then I'll see what I can do to make that happen."

"Be very careful, Ms. Sweet. You've been lucky so far, but Albert won't give up. He's become my worst nightmare. He could become yours, too."

CHAPTER TWELVE

The ice and blowing snow made for slow driving back into Ottawa. On the plus side, the snow had nearly stopped falling when I reached the west end of the city. I stopped at the store and picked up Evan's gift on my way home. I left the present safely set up in Nick's house and drove over to get Evan from his friend's place.

"Grandpa left some food in the freezer for supper," I said as he climbed into the passenger seat. "Would you like to drive downtown and look at the Christmas lights after we eat? The weather is clearing up."

"Yippee!" he yelled.

"I take that as a yes."

I parked in our driveway and Evan ran ahead of me to the front door. He waited for me to unlock it, but the door swung open under my hand. *Had I forgotten to lock it?*

"I'll go in first," I said.

The house was still and dark, as I'd left it. I walked down the hall, checking rooms along the way. Evan stayed near the front door and I heard him call me. I hurried back. Albert Romaine towered above Evan in the front hallway. He was larger than I remembered ... and more unhappy.

"You've been out," he said. "Have you something to report about Shelley?" His hair was wild-looking, and matched his eyes.

"Evan, why don't you go to your room and read the newspaper?" I asked.

Evan looked at me, his eyes wide. "Okay," he said, and raced past me before Albert could react.

I found my firm voice. "No, I have nothing to report. What are you doing here, Albert?"

"You've been gone all day. Did you meet her?"

"Are you following me?"

"I want to know where she is." He moved further into the entranceway and shut the door.

"Get out of my house," I said.

"I don't think so. Not until you tell me where she is." He took two steps in my direction. I backed up, feeling my way along the wall toward the kitchen. "She's a liar, you know. I paid you to find her and you have to tell me what you found out."

"You tried to break into my office," I said calmly. "You put a tracking device on my car."

"So what if I did? Prove it. How many vehicles do you own, anyhow?"

"I'm not working for you anymore, Mr. Romaine. I'll return your money. Get out of my house."

"Not until you tell me where she is. I know you met her."

He lunged at me and grabbed my arm. I hit him in the chest with my fist and he punched me in the face. I would have fallen over but he kept hold of me. Blood was pouring from my nose. "Tell me where she is," he said.

"I'm charging you with assault."

His face went a dark shade of purplish red and he was shaking with anger. He pushed me into the wall. "I'll kill you if you don't tell me where she is," he hissed.

I heard Evan on the stairs and pulled myself upright. I couldn't let him near Evan. "Get out ... of ... my ... house," I said through clenched teeth.

"Aunt Anna!" Evan yelled from above us. His voice was terrified.

Albert looked upstairs and back at me. "Tell me where she is or I'm taking the kid."

The next few moments seemed to unfold in slow motion. The front door swung open behind Albert with a blast of cold air. Jimmy charged into the hall right behind it, his eyes taking in the scene in front of him. He didn't hesitate and tackled Albert from behind, slamming him into the floor.

After much grunting and thumping, Jimmy managed to pin Albert in a stranglehold. He kept his full weight on Albert and twisted his arm behind his back until he stopped resisting.

Breathing heavily, Jimmy looked up at Evan. "You okay, bud?"

When Evan nodded, Jimmy turned his head to look at me, propped up against the wall. "You okay too, Sweet?"

"Never better."

Jimmy barked out a laugh. "You and Evan have quite the signal worked out. He texted me and then called 911. I was already on my way here from the airport in a cab, coming to pick him up."

As if to confirm what Jimmy said, I heard a siren off in the distance getting closer.

"Our 'read a newspaper' signal." I smiled and tilted my head back to stop the blood flowing from my nose. It didn't feel broken but maybe that was my wishful thinking.

Albert screamed and bucked like a wild animal, trying to push Jimmy off him. "Let me go!" he screeched.

Jimmy slammed Albert into the floor again. "You're not going anywhere but a jail cell," he said, putting both knees on Albert's back and bearing down. "Anna's going to fill me in on what you've been up to."

"The list is long," I said. "Break and enter. Two assaults, one with a weapon. Threatening to kidnap and kill ... I think we have enough to put this bully away for a good long time."

CHAPTER THIRTEEN

As it turned out, I wasn't alone Christmas morning. Jimmy spent the night on the couch and Evan woke us both up to open all the presents that we'd managed to get under the tree after visiting the hospital. He was thrilled with the telescope from Dad and the new downhill skis from Jimmy. I kept my gift hidden until the last minute, sneaking out a few times to check on it. Then I brought Evan and Jimmy to Nick's house with me.

Seven-month-old Sammy was snoozing in the kitchen. But he jumped up when he saw us, tail wagging like a flag.

"Is he really mine?" Evan kept repeating.

"He is, and Grandpa says he can live with us if neither your mom nor your dad has room. We'll all help look after him."

"A beagle?" asked Jimmy.

"Yup. From the animal shelter."

"My very own dog."

Jimmy waited until we were in the kitchen making breakfast to say, "Stroke of genius giving him a dog, Sweet. Thanks."

"Cheri might not be as thrilled but Sammy can stay with us."

"I'll take him when Evan's with me. We'll make it work."

"Why did you cut your holiday in Cuba short?" I asked.

Jimmy's eyes met mine. "I checked my messages and found out Cheri was stuck in Barbados because of a storm. I realized that I wanted to be with family for Christmas."

"Well, Evan and I are certainly happy you came home when you did."

I slipped away to my room after breakfast and called Nick using a video app. He was shocked at the sight of my bruised nose and blackened eyes.

"You should see the other guy," I said, stealing a line from Gino. I filled him in on what had happened.

"Is this Albert Romaine under arrest?" asked Nick, his face as angry as I'd ever seen it.

"He is, with a list of charges a mile long. Gino and I are both pressing charges. We're asking Shelley if she wants to come forward as well with her story. She recorded some of his abuse and it can be used in court."

"I hope they throw the book at him."

"Me too."

After a few moments, Nick's eyes softened. "I miss you."

"I'm waiting for you to come home to give you my Christmas present," I said.

"You can give it to me in two days, then. We're wrapping up early and I've booked a flight. Let's make this the last Christmas we're apart from each other."

I laughed. "We can try, but I suspect our lives are never going to be that predictable."

He tilted his head and smiled. "But I *can* predict that life is never going to be boring with you around, Anna Sweet."

ABOUT THE AUTHOR

ALAN DEAN

Brenda Chapman is a well-known mystery author. The Anna Sweet Mysteries are a popular series in adult literacy and English as a Second Language programs. *My Sister's Keeper*, the first title in the series, was a finalist for the Arthur Ellis Award in 2014. *The Hard Fall* was nominated for the Golden Oak Award in 2014. A former teacher and senior communications advisor, Brenda makes her home in Ottawa.

ALSO BY BRENDA CHAPMAN

In Winter's Grip   *Butterfly Kills*
The Second Wife   *Tumbled Graves*
Second Chances   *Shallow End*
Cold Mourning

Anna Sweet Mysteries

My Sister's Keeper
The Hard Fall
To Keep a Secret
A Model Death
No Trace

Jennifer Bannon Mystery Series

Running Scared
Hiding in Hawk's Creek
Where Trouble Leads
Trail of Secrets

You can visit Brenda's website at www.brendachapman.ca